My Parents Still Love Me

Even Though

They're Getting Divorced

(an interactive tale for children)

My Parents Still Love Me

Even Though

They're Getting Divorced

(an interactive tale for children)

Written by Lois V. Nightingale, Ph.D.

Artwork by Blanca Apodaca

Published by:

Nightingale Rose Publications
16960 E. Bastanchury Rd. Ste. J
Yorba Linda, Ca. 92886

Published by Nightingale Rose Publications,
16960 E. Bastanchury Rd., Suite I, Yorba Linda, Ca. 92886.

Artwork by Blanca Apodaca

Printed and bound in the United States of America

Library of Congress Catalog Card Number: 96-92679

Summary: A fantasy story and workbook to educate, support and help
children and their families going through divorce.
Literary bibliography included.
1997 first printing
2005 second printing

ISBN 1-889755-00-1

Disclaimer
This book is designed to provide information in regard to the subject matter covered. It is not designed to take the place of professional counseling. If an adult or a child is having a
particularly difficult time handling changes they are facing, it is important to seek professional help. If a child or an adult is experiencing signs of depression, severe anxiety reactions, or
other severe psychological disturbances, it is important that to receive professional psychological help. Licensed therapists in your area can be found through the yellow pages of your local
°phone company under "Psychologists", "Marriage therapy", or "Psychiatry". Local psychiatric hospitals also give free referrals to persons requesting psychological assistance.

This book is dedicated to my children,
Harry and Teddi,
to my father, my forever
knight in shining armor,
and to all the parents who are struggling
with the complex challenges of helping
the children they love through divorce.

Contents

Acknowledgments

I wish to extend a special acknowledgment to all the non-custodial parents who sacrifice daily to meet the financial and emotional commitments to the children they love, in spite of possible animosity toward their other parent. Your gifts to your children have a great impact on their future, the future of our world, and will be returned to you many times over.

An important note to parents, counselors, educators and librarians:

Useful suggestions for reading and using this book:

Parents

It is suggested that the child's parent(s), or other supportive adult, read this book first, before presenting it to the child. Many concepts presented in the story require adult support and further explanation. For a child to have greatest benefit from the story and activities, it is strongly recommended that an adult read to, or along with the child.

When dealing with information that may elicit strong emotions, children may have a shorter attention span than while watching TV or playing a video game. It is important not to rush kids through the story or the experience of doing the workbook pages. Children may prefer to hear the story and do the activities in sections, rather than all in one sitting. Many parents prefer to read through the entire story once (usually in parts, over 2-3 days) and then have children fill in the workbook pages upon a second reading. This allows a child to first understand that other children have gone through a similar experience and have come out all right. Children may feel freer to express their ideas and feelings if they know everything will turn out all right in the end.

It is also important to let the child know there are no "right" or "wrong" answers, and that there will be no judgments or criticisms made about their responses. Parents can let a child know they are free to do as many or as few of the workbook pages as they feel comfortable doing. Coloring the picture pages first may be a good introduction to having children write in this book.

Not all questions will be equally applicable to all children. Parents are encouraged to emphasize the areas which are pertinent to their child, and briefly read over, or skip altogether, the areas that do not pertain to the child's circumstances. If a child or family is having a particularly difficult time dealing with the emotions surrounding divorce, counseling may be very beneficial. This book is not meant to replace professional counseling for children.

Many children may be resistant at first to read about such a difficult topic; others will be excited that their silent questions will be answered. If your child appears resistant to reading this book with you, you may want to read sections of it during times when they are already feeling relaxed and comfortable (before reading their regular book at bed time, while they are in the bath tub, while you are rubbing their back before they go to sleep, while listening to relaxing music, outdoors at a park, while they are eating dessert, etc.)

If your child becomes bored, upset, or agitated during reading, you may want to ask them how they are feeling. (Some children are more comfortable "showing" how they feel, such as drawing a picture, doing a short skit, demonstrating with dolls or hitting a pillow.) And then, if they wish, let them know it is O.K. to put the book away for a while and come back to it later on or the next day.

Much of how a child reacts to changes in a family is dependent upon how they see their parents reacting. Be gentle, patient and kind to yourself. Most of us did not exhibit the communication skills used by the parents in this make-believe story, but we did the best that we could. Children will respond very positively when parents are self-forgiving and model how to be patient and loving to one's self.

If your child is too young to write in the workbook pages, he or she may draw pictures or representations of answers. You may also write in the answers said aloud for you.

Make sure your child has drawing and writing materials available as you work through the activities together. If there is more than one child in your family, you may want to provide each with a separate piece of paper and write the question(s) at the top of each page, or order a separate book for each child to write private thoughts in (ordering information is provided at the end of the book).

Remember, this book is not designed for a marathon course in divorce for children. Be very patient and gentle with a child going through this process. Your attitude of acceptance, regardless of your child's responses or how fast or slow he or she chooses to work through this book, is very important in helping attain the greatest possible benefit from this activity.

The story and activities provide an opportunity to become closer to your child. Completing two or three pages a day will give your child a better understanding of the divorce process, and let your child know he or she is important to you and that you will be there to help through this difficult time.

Counselors and therapists
Counselors and therapists may want to use this book to facilitate working with children going through a divorce or dealing with feelings after a divorce is final. It is suggested that the story and activities be presented in sections over the course of 3-5 therapy sessions, for the reasons outlined above. The fantasy story, coloring and workbook pages can provide a non-threatening approach to help children access their feelings about their parents separating. Therapists have also found working with this book can aid in diagnosing areas where a child may be having difficulty in coping with divorce.

This book also lends itself well to working with children in groups who are dealing with their parents' divorce. Once again, it is important to emphasize that there are no "right" or "wrong" answers. Group interaction and cohesiveness can be facilitated by using the workbook activities and having children share their own ideas (if they feel comfortable) with the rest of the group. Group art projects, children's own stories, poems and skits can add new dimensions to the ideas presented here, and help children develop a sense of understanding and empowerment.

Teachers and educators

Often a divorce can create disturbances in school behavior for children. If there are a number of children in a class that are experiencing this transition, using this book in the classroom can help demystify divorce, and remove the stigma that some children feel during this type of change. Children going through their parent's divorce may feel uncomfortable being identified personally, but may be relieved when information is presented to the entire class. With parent's permission, teachers may also wish to work with children individually using this book.

When used by teachers and educators, it is suggested that the book be read aloud once, and then again in sections, using the workbook pages to facilitate class discussion. The story may also be used to inspire creative art ideas, plays, or journaling projects for children.

Divorce is a painful reality in our world, one which few children are equipped to deal with. Teachers and educators may be the only adults children know who are not caught up in the emotional upheaval of the divorce. This may place the teacher in a unique position to assist children in a positive way and build self-esteem.

Teachers may also find that using this book to help facilitate talking about feelings may assist them in identifying children who need to be referred to the school psychologist. The recommend reading lists may be suggested to parents who need further resources.

Librarians

Libraries may be the greatest resource for children from single parent homes where finances are tight. Even though this book is presented in a workbook format, it lends itself well to facilitating verbal responses from children when working with a supportive adult. Children may also draw or write their answers on a separate sheet of paper. Libraries may wish to use this book as a reference, or encourage adult supervision.

How life once was

There once was a beautiful mermaid, from the depths of the ocean blue, and a noble knight from a mountain castle. They fell in love and decided to get married.

After they were married, they decided to live by the sea where they could hear the waves against the shore and where it would sing their babies to sleep. Being near the water, the mermaid could keep her skin wet so her beautiful iridescent scales would not dry out. But it was also above the water so the knight could breathe air, because he could not breathe under the water. It was a wonderful place for a home, where he could ride horses and she could make necklaces of sea shells.

The first few years were wonderful. The knight enjoyed the sea air, the sounds of the waves, and finding beautiful coral. It was so different from his home on the mountain where he grew up. The mermaid also enjoyed her new home. She was fascinated by watching the wind blow fluffy white clouds, birds flying and colorful sunsets. She had never seen any of these under the sea, where she grew up.

♥ The knight and the mermaid got married because they fell in love.

♥ Why do you think people get married?

During these years they had four beautiful children. The oldest was Constance, a lovely, helpful girl; next came Newton, a bright boy who loved to ask questions, then came Arletta, a sweet girl who loved animals and stories, and the youngest was Spartacus, an energetic boy who was always busy from early morning until late at night. Both the mermaid and the knight enjoyed their children very much!

♥ Do you know a story about your birth or a story about you when you were a tiny baby?

(If not, ask one of your parents or grandparents to tell you one.)

Each of the children had the very best traits of both their mother and father. They could swim under the water and breathe just like fish, and they could breathe air just like their father, the knight. They could go for long visits to their grandparents' home in the castle on the mountain, ride horses and never worry about their skin drying out. They could also visit their grandparents under the sea, for they were as at home in the ocean as were the fish. They were beautiful and handsome just like their parents. The mermaid and the knight loved their children very much and were very proud of all of them.

♥ The children could swim underwater like their mother.

♥ In what ways are you like your mother?

♥ The children could ride horses like their father.

♥ In what ways are you like your father?

Then trouble came

But one day, very dark clouds came over their home by the sea. The darkness became so thick that the flowers and the fruit trees died. The grass turned brown. And all the fields of grain dried up. The children could see that both their parents were very upset about the darkness.

At night they would hear their father talking in an angry voice saying that he missed the pine trees and the snow in the winter in the mountains. And their mother, also in an angry voice, would say that she missed the starfish and beautiful coral, and gliding free in the water. She felt her movements were so confined on land! Each one blamed the other for what they were missing!

♥ The children could hear their parents fighting.

♥ What did you do when you heard your parents fighting?

♥ Did anyone ever have to come and help them stop fighting (police, neighbors, relatives)?

As time went on, the angry voices grew louder at night. Their parents seemed to get madder and madder. The knight would say he wanted the family to move to the mountains and the mermaid would argue that they should all move into the sea.

As their parents became more and more angry with each other, they seemed to find more and more things to be upset about. Every little thing seemed to upset them, and they always seemed to find something to complain about to each other.

Sometimes there was just icy cold silence between them. The children felt sad when their parents fought and were scared when they could feel the silent anger in their home.

♥ The children could hear their parents becoming more and more angry.

♥ What things did you notice before your parents got divorced?

♥ How did you feel about these things?

One day, after seeing her mother so upset and grumpy, Constance asked her mother if she was mad at *her*. Her mother seemed a little surprised. She sat down on a chair and pulled Constance toward her.

"Things are very difficult right now, Dear. But I want you to know that I'm not angry with you. Sometimes things are overwhelming and I know I have not been a lot of fun lately or been very patient with you and your brothers and sister," said her mother.

"What could I do to help?" asked Constance.

"Dear, the things that are upsetting me are adult things. They don't have anything to do with you children. I appreciate you doing your chores and finishing your homework, but there is nothing you can do to fix the adult problems that your father and I are talking about. And I'll always love you," replied her mother.

Constance felt sad. She wanted so much to fix the bad feelings in her family. She felt relieved the troubles were not about her or her brothers or sister, but she did not like that there was nothing she could do to make it better. So she went for a walk along the beach and took food to feed the seagulls. It still felt strange because of the dark gloominess.

♥ Constance thought her mother was angry with her.

♥ Tell about a time you thought your parents were fighting about something that you did.

♥ Did you ask them what they were fighting about?

♥ What did they say?

A couple of days later, when their father came home, Spartacus was roughhousing. He was pretending he was a knight slaying a mighty dragon. Just as his father closed the front door, the big lamp in the living room came crashing down as Spartacus' pretend sword accidentally sent it flying.

CRASH! CLUNK! BANG! And then there was silence.

Spartacus looked up. His eyes were as wide as full moons. He looked at his father's face. It was red!

"Go to your room now!" yelled his father. His father, who was usually playful and funny, yelled at him all the way to his bedroom.

♥ Spartacus' father punished him by yelling at him and sending him to his room.

♥ Who usually punished you when your parents were together?

♥ How did they punish you?

♥ How did you feel about that?

Spartacus waited for what seemed like forever alone in his room. He was afraid. He had never heard his father so angry with him before. He could hear angry blaming voices coming from the other room, and then it was quiet. There came a quiet knock on the door, and his father came in.

"I'm sorry, Son," said the knight. "I am disappointed that you broke the lamp, and you know the rule about roughhousing in the house. But that was no excuse for how I yelled at you. There are other things on my mind and sometimes it's hard for me to be patient with unexpected problems."

Spartacus was confused. He didn't know what to do. A part of him wanted to be very angry and yell and scream; that way, maybe his father would blame him and stop thinking about his other problems.

"You're never any fun anymore! And you never play with me!" yelled Spartacus.

"I know you're upset and angry, Son," replied his father. "I wish I felt more like playing too. I wish I didn't have such a short temper right now. One day soon I will be back to my happy self, but right now things are very difficult for me. But please keep telling me how you feel. It's important to me. I may not always like what you tell me, but that's OK. None of us like how things are right now."

♥ Spartacus' father said he wanted to hear how his son was feeling even if his feelings were not always easy for him to hear.

♥ These are some feelings that kids may have.   ♥ Circle feelings you have had.

In-between feelings:

PLEASANT FEELINGS:

UNPLEASANT FEELINGS:

PLEASANT FEELINGS:			In-between feelings:	UNPLEASANT FEELINGS:			
AMUSED	BETTER	TRIUMPHANT	mischievous	confused	nervous	frightened	hurt
GREAT	EXCITED	SUCCESSFUL	apathetic	left out	suspicious	hopeless	sick
CONFIDENT	ENJOYABLE	DETERMINED	sleepy	depressed	resentful	unhappy	angry
ENCOURAGED	GRATEFUL	BALANCED	nostalgic	incapable	enraged	greedy	bored
HELPFUL	CAPABLE	FORGIVING	tempted	dissatisfied	grieving	sulky	lonely
SATISFIED	GOOD	JOYFUL	undecided	two-faced	clumsy	regretful	sad
INFATUATED	BLISSFUL	CONTENTED	conniving	bashful	agonized	aggressive	cranky
DEMURE	THOUGHTFUL	LOVED	timid	nauseated	accused	exhausted	guilty
GLAD	ECSTATIC	EFFICIENT	shocked	disapproving	overworked	miserable	envious
ACCEPTED	RELAXED	HAPPY	boastful	inadequate	embarrassed	forgetful	hostile
ENTHUSIASTIC	CREATIVE	PROUD	smug	argumentative	threatened	worthless	tired
HOPEFUL	PLEASED	COMFORTABLE	scheming	sorrowful	disgusted	put down	negative
IRRESISTIBLE	RELIEVED	SYMPATHETIC	indecisive	disrespectful	obstinate	homesick	anxious
NOBLE	OPTIMISTIC	SURPRISED	passive	defeated	miserable	pressured	difficult
TENDER	CONTENTED	CARING	skeptical	discouraged	overwhelmed	hysterical	frustrated
INDUSTRIOUS	SPIRITED	INNOCENT	exercised	disappointed	contemptuous	horrified	surly
PROUD	DELIGHTED	GRACEFUL	cautious	domineering	hopeless	competitive	scared
IMPRESSED	EAGER	GIGGLY	indifferent	rejected	vulnerable	exasperated	helpless
LOVABLE	APPRECIATED	NURTURING	apologetic	fiendish	unhappy	unfair	useless
AFFECTIONATE	EXPECTANT	RESPECTED	nonchalant	miserable	aggravated	jealous	worried
INSPIRED	ACCEPTED	CONCENTRATING	interested	unloved	insignificant	paranoid	insecure
COMPETENT	MELLOW	DETERMINED	perplexed	domineering	withdrawn	foolish	threatened

Newton had overheard the whole thing. He felt **very** uncomfortable. He especially didn't like to hear fighting. It made him feel sick in his stomach. He wished so much that things would be calm and happy again. He turned the volume up on his video game, and sat a little closer to the screen because the darkness made it harder to see.

♥ When Newton felt very uncomfortable his stomach hurt.

♥ When you feel upset do you ever have stomachaches?

Headaches?

♥ How does your body feel when you are angry?

♥ How does your body feel when you are happy?

♥ How does your body feel when you are sad?

♥ How does your body feel when you are afraid?

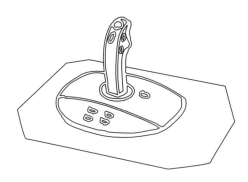

♥ How does your body feel when you are excited?

When Arletta heard all the noise, she went to her special place (a hidden corner in her room) and began to draw a picture of a very angry dragon breathing fire. She used a bright red crayon and a black one to make big black clouds in the sky.

♥ Arletta has a special place she likes to go to be alone.

♥ Do you have a special place you like to go to think?

(Tree house, bedroom, backyard, secret hiding place...)

Mom and Dad tell the kids

The children had noticed that their parents were spending less and less time together. Sometimes one of them would leave for a few days and then come back home. The children felt confused and frightened as life went on this way. Everyone was so sad and angry all the time. The children hoped that things would get better, because they so wanted things to be different!

♥ As the mermaid and the knight fought more and more sometimes one of them would leave for a while.

♥ If your parents separated before they decided to divorce, how did you feel during that time? (You can use the lists of feeling words on page 29.)

One night, after dinner, the knight and the mermaid called all the children into the living room. Everyone sat down. The children could sense that something serious was going to be talked about. (Kids always know that kind of stuff.)

Constance retied her shoelaces to perfectly match, and then sat perfectly still with her hands in her lap. Newton had his head buried in a book he had brought with him. Spartacus squirmed and eventually slid off the couch and laid down on the floor with his feet up on the couch. Arletta moved a little to the side so his swinging feet didn't hit the cat she was gently holding in her lap.

There was a strange tension in the air as their father began to speak, "Your mother and I have something to tell you, and it is very difficult for us," he began.

Newton looked over the top of the book he was reading, and even Spartacus looked upside-down at his father.

"Your father and I have decided that we can no longer live together," said their mother.

"Are you getting divorced?" Spartacus blurted out.

"Spart! Be quiet!" snapped Constance.

"Yes, it looks like we will be getting a divorce," said their father. "And it's all right to ask any questions you may have. We will answer them the best we can. Some things we don't have figured out yet. But all of your questions are important to us."

♥ The children were told about the divorce by both their parents. Sometimes only one parent tells the children, or sometimes someone else does.

♥ Who told you your parents were getting divorced?

♥ Did you feel……

sad	worried	ignored	happy	nervous
guilty	angry	confused	ashamed	frightened
safe	scared	trapped	curious	apprehensive
uncertain	lonely	embarrassed	hurt	disappointed
_____	_____	_____	_____	_____

(You can look back to page 29 for more feeling words.)

"Don't you love each other anymore? Don't you love us anymore?" Arletta could barely choke out the words.

"Your father and I can no longer live together," answered their mother. "But no matter how we feel about each other we will always love you, no matter what."

Does this mean we won't be a family anymore?" asked Constance.

"Well," began their mother, "You might want to think of yourselves as belonging to **two** families now. But you will always be our children and we will always do our best to make sure that you are taken care of."

"If you are scared or confused as these changes are happening, it's important for you to talk to someone you feel really listens. Your father and I will try to be there for you to talk to, and I know your grandparents are interested in your thoughts and feelings. You may have friends at school whose parents are divorced and you might feel comfortable talking to them. I know you're very close to Aunt Judi, and you could call her and ask her to take you out for ice cream, if you would like to talk with her."

"There are also counselors who help kids talk about their feelings and learn to feel safe. It's important for you to know, that even though our family is changing, you still have a lot of people around you who care about you and will listen to you."

♥ Constance has many choices of people to talk to.

♥ Who do you like to talk to when you feel bad?

__ a special friend   __ your mother   __ your father

__ a teacher   __ a counselor   __ a coach

__a rabbi   __ a minister   __ a priest

__ a grandparent   __ an aunt   __ an uncle

__ your baby-sitter   __a cousin   __ one of your parent's friends

__ a pet   __ a stuffed animal   _____

"Where will we live? Who will take care of us? Will we have to move? Do Grandma and Grandpa know? Why do you want a divorce?" Constance appeared very upset and began crying.

"Dear, it's O.K. to be upset about this; we're all sad. It's O.K. to cry and it's all right to be frightened. Your father and I will always make sure that you're taken care of. You will spend some of your time with me and some of your time with your father. You will always be with someone who loves you very much," replied their mother.

"There's not a simple answer to why we're getting a divorce," their father said. "But you must know it has nothing to do with you children. This is a grown-up decision, and it's about grown-up things. There's nothing you children did that caused this and there's nothing that you can do that will get us back together again."

Constance couldn't imagine living separately from either of her parents. How would her parents feel when she hugged and kissed the other one good-bye? Did either of her parents want her to take sides against the other one? She felt very confused.

♥ Constance felt frightened and confused. It was hard for her to imagine living at two different houses and spending time alone with each parent.

♥ It is normal to feel confused when your parents are getting divorced. What were some things that you found confusing?

♥ It is all right to keep loving both your parents.

♥ Does it now feel strange to show one parent that you loved them in front of the other?

Newton had retreated behind his book again.

"Any questions, Newt?" asked his father.

"My friend Jake's father is a sailor, and he went away forever. Are you going to do that?" he asked as he peered over the top of his book.

"No," his father replied. "I know some parents feel so guilty or so sad that they don't call or come to see their children because it's too hard for them. And I may be very hurt and very sad about the divorce, but I will not do that. I plan to see you a lot. You can call me any time you are at your mother's home, and you can call her any time you are with me. Both of us will always be part of your life. We both love you very much."

♥ Newton was glad that his father would still spend time with him, but he knew there would be times when he would be away from his father.

♥ It is not always easy to be away from someone you love.

♥ What are ways you can keep in touch with the parent you are not with?

__ write notes   __ draw pictures

__ send school work and art   __ write poems

__ write stories   __ collect jokes they might like

__ phone calls   __ cell phone / text messaging

__ start a scrap book   __ webcam conversations

__ have a picture of them in your room   __ voice mail

__ give them a picture of you   __ E-mail / Instant Messaging

__ make a recording of your voice   __ make a home video of yourself

__ let them know about up-coming school events   _____

"If we move can we bring Kitty Cat with us?" asked Arletta.

"She'll be able to stay at your home with your father," replied their mother. "At my house you might prefer to get a new catfish, or maybe a dolphin."

"What if you two can't agree on who will take care of us?" Arletta asked.

"There are people who will help us decide," replied her father. "We may see a mediator who helps people find answers to these kinds of questions. If that doesn't work, we will each have an attorney, and they will help us decide. If we still can't agree then a judge will listen to both sides and then decide what will happen. The judge will make the final decision, and everyone has to obey those rules."

♥ There are some things parents may need help in deciding:

Visitation: How much time children will spend with the parent they don't usually live with.

Physical Custody: The parent who has Physical Custody is the parent the kids live with the most. Joint Physical Custody means both parents share time with the children equally.

Legal Custody: The parent who has Legal Custody makes decisions about what schools and what doctors children go to. Joint Legal Custody means both parents share in these decisions.

Child Support: Money one parent gives to the other to help pay for things children need.

Spousal Support: Money one parent gives the other to help them out until they can make enough money on their own.

♥ Which of these things did your parents have trouble making decisions about?

"Can I leave now!?" Spartacus asked rudely.

"Yes, Son, I think that is enough for now. But as each of you has questions I hope you will come to either one of us and ask. And if it seems too hard to talk to us, remember there are other people who would also be happy to help you," said their mother.

The children all seemed relieved that the "talk" was over. Constance went over to her mother and climbed into her lap. Spartacus grabbed his ball and mitt and slammed the door on his way outside. Newton took his book and went to his room and turned on a video game. Arletta took Kitty Cat and walked outside and sat where the garden used to be before it got so dark.

♥ Who helped your parents with their divorce?

__ Clergy (rabbi, priest, minister, reverend, bishop)

__ Counselor or therapist (A person trained to help people talk about their feelings)

__ Mediator (a person who helps parents divide belongings, money, and time with children)

__ Attorney (lawyer) (a person who gives your parents advice about dividing things up, and may talk to the judge for your parent)

__ Judge (the person who makes the final decision about how things are divided up, and which parent takes care of the children. The judge is the person who says the divorce is final, and both parents are free to marry again)

♥ Did you have your own attorney (lawyer)?   ♥ If so, how did you feel about him or her?

♥ Did the judge want to talk to you?

♥ If so, did you do the best you could to answer the judge's questions as honestly as you could?

♥ Did you have to wait a long time in court?   ♥ What did you do while you waited?

♥ Has the judge written out the rules and signed a paper saying that the divorce is final yet?

The children's reactions

SPARTICUS

As Spartacus stomped down the sidewalk that ran along the beach, he could feel rage building inside him. "It's not fair!" he thought. "No one asked **me** if **I** wanted Mom and Dad to get divorced!"

He felt his heart racing as he began to get more and more angry. He kicked a stick that was on the walk in front of him. He hit his mitt hard with his baseball. He wanted to scream and yell. Then he thought that if he was really bad, maybe his Mom and Dad would have to stay together to keep him in line, and they would see how much he wanted them to stay together.

♥ Draw a picture of how you felt when you found out your parents were going to get divorced.

Spartacus ran back home and burst through the door. He threw his ball at the door and screamed, "I hate you! You don't love me anymore!"

His father looked very surprised. "Spartacus, come here, Son!" he said in a stern voice. "Tell me what is going on. You sound very angry."

"I am mad! I am mad at you and Mom and everybody!" Spartacus yelled.

His father sat down on the floor and motioned for his son to sit next to him. Spartacus just stood there with his arms crossed, staring at the wall, with tears running down his cheeks.

"Son," the knight continued anyway, "I know you're upset and angry. It's all right to feel angry, sad, and disappointed. It's even O.K. to tell me about it. I always love you, even when you are angry and hurt. But I don't approve of you throwing things in the house. It's not all right to express your anger in ways that might hurt people or things. Can you think of other ways you might be able to get your anger out?"

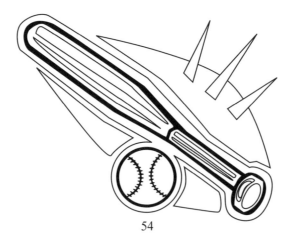

♥ Spartacus was very angry. Some of the ways he showed he was mad were O.K.; but other ways were not.

♥ What ways would you like to use to help get your angry feelings out?

__ Talk to someone   __ Run   __ Draw pictures

__ Write stories   __ Dance   __ Hit clay

__ Punch a punching bag   __ Exercise   __ Jump on a trampoline

__ Shoot baskets   __ Listen to music   __ Yell into a pillow

__ Hit a pillow   __ Jump   __ Play video games

__ Say really angry words alone with your door closed   __ Walk the dog

__ Throw a ball   __ Play a musical instrument

__ Cry   __ Have someone hold you

__ Write an angry feeling on a rock and throw it into a lake, river or ocean.

__ Write down angry feelings and then stomp on the paper or poke holes in it.

"How about if we go outside and play catch and I throw the ball real hard?" Spartacus said half angry, and half hoping his father would play with him.

"Well, if you're calm enough to aim well, so I don't have to chase it," his father laughed. "Would you like to hit the punching bag with me first to get some of that frustration out before we play catch?"

"Well, all right," he said as they headed outside.

"You know your Mother and I aren't getting divorced because of anything you've done don't you?"

"Yeah," he mumbled.

"And there is also nothing you can do to get us to stay together."

Spartacus looked up surprised. "How did you know about that?" he asked.

♥ Spartacus was glad his father helped him think of things he could do when he was upset. He especially liked doing things with his father.

♥ What are some things you like to do with your dad?

"Well, lots of kids hope they can get their parents back together," his father replied. "Some kids think they can get their parents to stay together by being extra good and helpful, other ones by acting out and making trouble."

"I bet Constance is being a 'Goody-two-shoes' for that reason. She makes me sick!" Spartacus replied.

"I know it's difficult for you to get along with your sisters under normal conditions. And I know that everyone has a shorter fuse when big changes are happening. But I would appreciate it if you found things to keep you busy and not fight with your sisters. We all handle this kind of change differently. Please be patient with all of us."

But by this time Spartacus had his gloves laced up and was growling and attacking the punching bag. His dad joined in.

♥ Spartacus talked to his father about how much his sister upset him.

♥ Was it more difficult to get along with a brother or sister during the time your parents were going through the divorce?

♥ What did your brother or sister do that REALLY bothered you?

CONSTANCE

After the family discussion Constance sat in her mother's lap for a while. She talked to her mother about how very much she wanted things to go back to the way they were.

"Aren't families supposed to stay together no matter what?" she asked her mother. "I'm never going to get a divorce when I grow up. I'm never going to make my children move or have to change from one family to two!"

"Things don't always work out the way we plan them, Dear," her mother replied "When you're a grown-up you will get to make the adult decisions in your own family. It's not always easy to figure out what is best. Your father and I have made many mistakes, but we have always done the very best things we could think of to do at the time. We've never been parents before," she said with a smile.

♥ Even though Constance usually felt she was too big to sit in her mother's lap, when she felt confused and angry she felt safer being held by her mother and talking with her.

♥ What things does your mother do that make you feel special and loved?

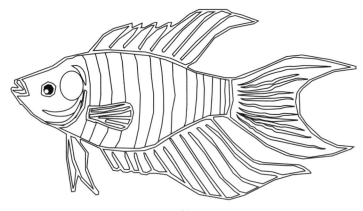

As the days went by Constance felt sad about the changes going on in her family. Sometimes she felt so sad that her head hurt. When she felt especially sad she went to talk to her counselor, Dr. Huggs. Dr. Huggs was always kind and she was always ready to hear what Constance had to say.

Dr. Huggs told Constance that what parents decide to do is up to them. She told Constance it was normal for kids to feel sad and angry when their parents divorce. She reminded Constance to do fun things for herself and not just try to take care of everyone else. But Constance still liked to keep her room neat and finish her homework on time; these things made her feel like she was helping herself to feel better.

♥ Constance found many things that helped her feel better.

♥ There are many things you can do to feel better:

Talk to a friend
Count slowly to ten
Play with clay
Paint a picture
Go swimming (with supervision)
Play with a pet
Dance
Watch animals
Pray to God
Make something for an upcoming holiday
Learn a new sport
Build or make something
Call someone you love
Visit a friend
Create a treasure hunt
Write on the sidewalk with chalk
Have someone take you to a park and feed the ducks
Make a special sandwich
Get or give a hug

Write a story
Breathe deeply
Go to the batting cages
Take a walk with someone
Play outdoors
Listen to music
Play sports
Rollerblade
Talk to your Guardian Angel
Play a video or computer game
Go skateboarding or bicycling
Read
Make a card for someone
Organize your room
Finger paint
Plant some seeds
Find animals in the clouds
Rent your favorite DVD
Watch fish

One day her mother began to complain to Constance about her father. "...and if only he would..." she began, but Constance interrupted her. "Mom, if you have something bad to say about Dad, you need to tell him or another adult. I don't want to hear bad things about either one of you." She remembered what her counselor had told her about telling her parents that she would not listen to either of them complain about the other one, and she would not carry messages back and forth between them.

"You're right," her mother said. "It must have been hard for you to tell me that. I appreciate you speaking up about how you feel when you hear bad things about one of your parents. I will try very hard not to say those kinds of things to you or your brothers or sister. And remember, even when I have bad feelings about your dad, I still love you."

♥ It was hard for Constance to tell her mother she didn't want to hear bad things about her father.

♥ Have either of your parents told you bad things about the other one?

♥ What did you say or do?

♥ What would you like your parents to do?

NEWTON

Things began to change more as they began packing to move. The house seemed so different now. There were still many arguments between their parents but the children were learning ways of feeling better.

Newton kept to himself much of the time. He had one close friend, Cassidy. Mostly they played computer games together and made up jokes. They didn't talk about the divorce, but Newton knew his friend cared about him, and that helped a lot.

♥ Newton found ways to help himself even though many changes were taking place.

♥ Did you have to move?

♥ Which of your parents moved out?

♥ Do both of your parents stay in contact with you?

♥ How do you feel about that?

Sometimes Newton would be very distracted at school and stare out the window, thinking. His teacher, Ms. Johnson, noticed this and asked him after school what was going on.

"Oh, nothing," he replied. But he knew he was really thinking about how out of control this all felt. He had been trying to make sense out of it all. He had even gone to the library and checked out books for kids on divorce. He felt surprised that people would decide to not be together because of arguing. He **liked** to argue with his friends, but they didn't get angry with each other. They thought it was **fun**! Why a divorce? Why a move? Why so much anger? Why? Why? Why?

♥ Newton wondered "why" about many parts of his parents' divorce.

♥ What things have you wondered WHY about?

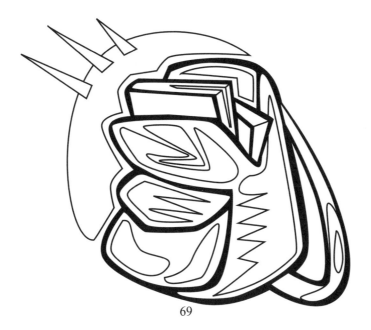

Again his teacher asked, "Anything wrong, Newt?"

"I just don't understand why my parents are getting a divorce. I wish they wouldn't fight so much, and my stomach hurts a lot," he blurted out.

"It is hard when we don't understand something," his teacher said. "I notice that you aren't playing with the other children."

"I just want to be left alone. I think over and over what my parents fight about and try to make sense out of it. If I try hard enough to figure it out I think I should understand it."

"Well, many things do work that way," his teacher smiled. "Like learning a new way to solve a math problem. But other things are not easily understood. In some cases we have to focus on figuring out what we can do to feel better, and not work so hard on figuring out the WHY."

"But I always like figuring out the WHY," Newton protested.

His teacher laughed, "I know you do, Newton. That's one of the things that makes you special. But I hope you spend as much time on figuring out how you can feel happy again. Sometimes we don't ever completely understand WHY."

She gave him a big hug, and he knew she really cared and did understand his confusion. That made him feel better, even if he didn't know exactly why.

♥ Newton was confused and frustrated at not having all the answers he wanted, and he also felt comforted by his teacher, even though he still felt confused.

♥ Sometimes people feel can feel two different feelings at once.

♥ It is O.K. to feel two different feelings at the same time.

Such as:

Surprised and Sad
Hopeful and Disappointed
Angry and Relieved
Loving and Mad

♥ What two different feelings have you felt?

_____and_____

_____and_____

_____and_____

ARLETTA

Arletta had been trying very hard over the past few weeks to keep peace in the family. She interrupted when she saw a fight coming on. And she tried to pretend she was happy. But as time went on she was becoming tired.

She spent more and more time in her room reading stories of far away places. She was just **sure** that everything was going to work out all right. She drew pictures of her whole family up in the castle on the mountain with a swimming pool for her mother. She drew pictures of the whole family under the sea living in a giant bubble for her father. She drew pictures of the sun coming out from behind the clouds at the beach where they lived now.

♥ Arletta wanted so much for things to go back the way they were. It is normal for kids to want their family back together, even when they know it will not happen.

♥ What things did you hope would get your parents back together or make things different?

♥ Who did you talk to about that?

She took the pictures to her mother, hoping to cheer her up. "Look what I made for you," she said.

The mermaid looked very pleased with her gifts. But as she looked closely at the pictures, her face grew serious. "This whole thing is very hard for you isn't it?" she asked.

Arletta shrugged. She didn't want her mother to feel bad for her.

"I know you wish this divorce was not happening and that everyone would feel better. It's a sad time for all of us. But your father and I have come to this decision because we hope, after a while we will both be happy again."

"But I wish you were both happy now. I can't stand to see you cry. I want everyone to be happy right now," she said softly.

♥ It was difficult for Arletta to see her parents sad and unhappy.

♥ Have you seen your parents cry?

♥ How do you feel when they cry?

♥ Do you know that crying can sometimes help even adults feel better?

"Remember the caterpillar you caught on the driftwood last spring?" her mother asked.

"Yes, I remember. He was fuzzy and green and moved like an accordion," she smiled.

"Remember when he made a cocoon and you couldn't see him inside of it?"

"Yes."

"And remember how much you wanted to open that cocoon and let him out?"

"Yes."

"Do you remember what I told you?"

"Yes, you said if I didn't wait for him to completely turn into a butterfly on his own, and come out when he was ready, that I could hurt him and he might never turn into a butterfly," she replied.

"That's right. And did he eventually come out on his own?"

"Yes! And he was beautiful!" she exclaimed.

"Well sometimes people's sadness is like that. We can't hurry it along or make it better for them," her mother said.

"Then one day you and Dad will be happy again?" she asked hopefully.

♥ Arletta's mother helped her understand about sadness by telling her a story.

♥ What things does your mother do that make you feel special and loved?

"Well that's what we're hoping for. We believe if we stay together we won't ever be happy again. We hope that after the divorce, each of us will be happy again in our own homes. We hope that you children will also be happier because we won't be fighting and we'll be more fun to be with."

"Not all parents are happy after divorce," said Arletta. "My friend Amy's mom and dad fought and yelled and even threw things at each other during the divorce. She saw her dad hurt her mom real bad one time. And now, even though their divorce is all over, her dad still isn't happy."

"It is true that some parents continue to fight even after a divorce and still stay mad at each other. When people carry a lot of anger around inside of them, it's hard for them to be happy. Some parents stay mad even though they know they must both share the children they had together."

"Some other parents may have an addiction to drugs or alcohol or another addiction. And if they don't get help for their addiction it can keep making them sad and the people around them unhappy."

"So how do you know that after you and Dad are divorced that you will not still be angry?' Arletta asked.

"That's up to me," her mother replied. "I have friends and a counselor who remind me that only I can decide to keep being angry or choose to let the anger go away."

♥ People may be addicted to many things. An addiction is being unable to stop doing something that hurts you. Some people have an addiction to drugs or alcohol. Other addictions may be gambling, spending too much money, eating too much food or often getting very angry.

♥ If you know someone with an addiction, draw a picture of what you think it looks like, or how it makes you feel:

"Do you think Dad will stop being so angry too?" Arletta asked.

"Well that's up to him. Neither you or I can make him feel any different than he feels. It's up to each of us to do things we feel good about," replied the mermaid.

"Yeah, and if we do things we feel bad about it's easier to get mad at someone else. Yesterday, when I accidentally broke Amy's new hair clip and didn't tell her, I felt bad," said Arletta. "And while I was feeling bad, Billy pushed me in line. I know it was an accident, but I got **really** mad and yelled at him and shoved him back. I know I did it because I was already feeling bad about not telling Amy about her hair clip."

♥ Arletta got angry very easily because she was already upset about something else.

♥ What things do you get angry about?

♥ Can you write about a time when you got mad easily because you were already feeling bad about something else?

"That's right. So what kinds of things would you like to do to feel better right now, while your father and I are going through this divorce?" her mother asked.

"Well I like to draw, and write stories. I also like to read. I like to talk to you and I like to play make-believe games with my friends. I like to play with animals and pretend they understand what I'm thinking and that they can talk back to me. I especially like playing with Kitty Cat," she replied.

"You have lots of creative ways to help yourself feel better! And you can take Kitty Cat's special bed to your father's house so you can always have it there when you visit," her mother reassured her.

Arletta sighed; she really hated that her parents were getting a divorce. She felt frightened and sad. But she was very sure of one thing: even though her parents were getting divorced, they still loved her.

♥ Draw a picture of yourself doing something that makes you feel better.

After they are settled

SPARTICUS

It felt strange living in new homes. Everything seemed different and unknown. But soon the children began to feel comfortable, especially Spartacus.

He had been very bored listening to the attorneys and he hated waiting in court! But now it was behind him he was ready for adventure!

When he spent time at his father's home he loved to explore in the woods with his toy sword. He liked to pretend that he was also a knight, rescuing anyone in trouble and fighting off fierce dragons.

He also liked having new things. He had new special sports equipment at each house. At his father's house he had his ball and mitt and a plastic disc he threw in the air, and a large flashlight to use at night in the forest.

♥ Spartacus liked having some of his things at his father's house.

♥ What special things of yours, do you have at your dad's house?

At his mother's house he had a ball and nets to play water polo, and a toy that made funny shaped bubbles of all colors to play with under the water, and a big searchlight to go exploring in underwater caves.

It was hard for Spartacus to get used to the different rules in each parent's house. He sometimes tried to talk one parent into letting him do something, by saying that the other parent would let him. But he found out that each parent had their own rules, and that the rules at each house had to be followed even if they were different. Anyway, he was already used to having different rules at school than at home.

Even though figuring out the different rules was hard, making friends was fun! Spartacus was the first to go looking for other kids in the neighborhoods. And soon he had new friends at both houses.

♥ Spartacus found that having new friends and special toys at each house helped him feel better.

♥ What special things of yours, do you have at your mom's house?

♥ What new friends have you made?

♥ What rules are different at each of your parents' homes?

Spartacus felt a little strange when he met his dad's new girlfriend. He tried to scare her by teasing her with a frog, but she just laughed and pretended it would turn into a prince if she kissed it. He thought she was silly! But she never tried to boss him around, and it was only up to his dad to tell him what to do. She was dad's friend, but he still liked to give her a hard time.

He also liked to spend time with each of his grandparents. The ones from the mountains took him to play in the snow, and showed him how to make a snowman, and have a snowball fight! The ones from the sea took him on adventures to see weird glowing fish and electric eels! (He liked that kind of stuff!)

Spartacus was learning that even when things change, there were still people to have fun with who loved him. And even though his parent were getting divorced, he was still very loved!

♥ Spartacus liked that his dad's new friend didn't try to tell him what to do.

♥ If you have met one of your parents' new friends, how did you feel?

♥ What did you do?

♥ Spartacus was lucky to have grandparents to play with him.

♥ What other adults, other than your parents, play with you?

CONSTANCE

Constance had a little harder time adjusting. She still missed her old house, but she liked spending more time close to each of her grandparents.

She could talk to one of her grandmas about the times her parents tried to put her in the middle of their arguments, and she would have to tell them to leave her out of it. She told her grandmother how very much she wanted her parents to get along and stop fighting, especially about money. They seemed to blame the other one for each of their money problems.

Sometimes she felt guilty. But her grandmother told her it was not her fault.

Even when her parents began to fight less, there still wasn't as much money as before the divorce. Now they did many fun things that didn't cost anything, instead of some of the things they used to do that took money. Mostly she didn't mind, she just liked to have fun. But sometimes she was disappointed when her mother said they couldn't afford to buy something that she really wanted.

♥ It was hard for Constance to hear her parents fight about money. Sometimes she was disappointed when she couldn't buy something she wanted.

♥ How do your parents spend money differently now that they are divorced?

♥ How do you feel about that?

♥ If your parents fight about money, how do you feel about that?

Another thing Constance didn't like was the extra chores the children had to help with now. She didn't mind so much doing her jobs, washing dishes and cleaning her room. But she was angry the other kids didn't help!

One day she talked to her mother about how unfair she felt it was. Her mother listened carefully to what she said. Then the mermaid decided to call a family meeting. She could see that not all the children were as willing to help as Constance.

At the family meeting the children chose chores they would like to help with. But the children told her it would be easier to remember to complete the chores if they were complimented and rewarded. Things were very different now and it was easy to forget that more help was needed.

"I have a great idea," their mother said. "Get your crayons and markers and meet me back here in the living room." They all sat down on the floor around a huge piece of cardboard she had found. Together they made a big chart. They all got to color it and remind their mother what chores each of them would do. Their mother promised to give them a gold star each time they finished one of the chores on the chart. They could then trade in the stars for an extra dessert, borrowing books at the library, or staying up later on weekend nights.

Constance felt better knowing she was not the only one helping out. She also liked that using the star chart her mother wasn't always yelling at Spartacus, reminding him to do his chores. But mostly Constance was happy that her mother took the time to listen to her concerns, and now, once a week, the family met for a "family meeting" to talk about their feelings, things they liked or didn't like during the week, and any changes they wanted in their chores.

♥ Constance found that when she talked to her mother about a problem that was bothering her, her mother listened to her.

♥ What problem have you talked about with your mom?

♥ How did you solve the problem?

♥ What problem have you talked about with your dad?

♥ How did you solve that problem?

♥ What problems would you still like to solve with your parents?

Constance kept special toys and books that she really liked at each of her houses. Her room at her father's house was smaller and she had to share it with her sister. But she kept her favorite doll there, and it was the first thing she ran to go see when she got to her father's house.

At her mother's house she liked to listen to the bubbles outside her window as she went to sleep at night. She had her favorite drawings up on the wall and liked the bright colors her room was painted.

♥ Constance found that there were special things at each of her parents' homes.

♥ Draw a picture of something special at your mom's house.

♥ Draw a picture of something special at your dad's house.

Sometimes things would remind Constance of the past and how things used to be. When she felt sad about this, she liked to call her friends and talk. She had one special friend from volleyball, whose parents were also divorced. Constance felt like she really understood how she felt. Constance was glad she had joined the team where she had met her new friend.

♥ What groups do you belong to?

__ school

__ scouts

__ band

__ sports

__ gymnastics

__ church

__ temple

_____

__ boy's and girl's club

__ chorus

__ equestrian

__ dancing

__ martial arts

__ computer class

__ special classes

_____

One of Constance's favorite things was to spend time alone with each parent. But because they were so busy, and there were so many kids, this didn't happen as often as she would have liked.

Her mother did try very hard to spend time alone with her, and do things she liked to do. She liked to paint her nails with her mother, and have her mother curl her hair. She liked it when her mother gave her a back rub, and when they baked cookies together. They even planted flower seeds together in an underwater garden. She loved to hear her mother tell stories of sea serpents and buried treasure. The special time she spent alone with each parent made Constance very happy!

Constance was learning that even though many things may change, some things remain the same. She knew her parents still loved her, even though they were getting divorced.

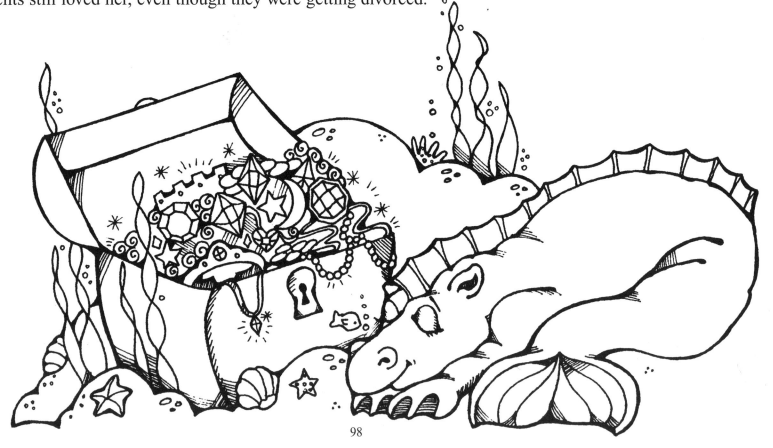

♥ One of the things Constance liked best was spending time alone with each
   parent.

♥ How often do you get alone time with each parent?

♥ If you asked, do you think you might be able to do a special activity with each of
   them?

♥ What is something that doesn't cost any money that you would like to do alone
   with one of your parents?
   (read a book, color, feed ducks at the park, watch trains or air planes, make up songs, go to the
   library, go to a museum, find constellations of stars at night, pick wildflowers, play a guessing
   game, play cards, tell jokes, sing, play hide and seek, have them tell you a story of
   when they were young.)

NEWTON

Newton was the first one to learn both the new phone numbers by heart. He also had a large collection of books and computer games at both houses. This made him feel "at home" wherever he was.

At first it seemed like his father was trying to get him to like his house better, by buying everything that Newton might want. Even though he liked to get presents, Newton thought maybe his father thought he only wanted to come to his house for the presents.

He finally told his father that he liked being at his house just so he could be with him. His father didn't have to keep buying him things so that Newton would love him. Newton just wanted to spend time with his father. (And he liked the presents!)

♥ Newton liked being able to call his parents when he wanted to.

♥ Write each of your parent's phone numbers.

♥ If you don't know the phone numbers by heart, who can help you find them or help you make the call?

♥ It was hard for Newton to talk to his dad about buying so many presents.

♥ Have either of your parents seemed like they were trying to get you to like being with them by buying you presents?

♥ If so, what would you like to tell them?

Newton continued to do well at his school, but he did it because *he* liked to, not because he thought it would keep his parents from fighting.

He still liked to spend time alone, and enjoyed his quiet time at both the houses.

♥ Newton did not have to change schools, but sometimes kids have to.

♥ Did you have to change schools?

♥ If so, was it hard or easy to make new friends?

♥ What new friends did you meet?

♥ Was it easy or hard to fit into the new classroom?

♥ Was your new class ahead or behind your old class?

♥ How did you feel about that?

Even though Newton kept to himself a lot, he watched everything that went on around him. He was glad that the fighting was less and that his parents seemed happier.

But there was one thing he really didn't like. Newton was very upset when he saw one of his parents doing something that was against the special rules the judge had made. (He knew the judge wanted what was best for kids.)

Once when his father took the children to a party he drank alcohol (which was against the rules the judge had made). Newton wrote a note to both his parents reminding them that the rules the judge made needed to be followed. He was afraid that they might be mad at him, but he didn't want to lose out on time with his father because he didn't follow the rules.

After he wrote the notes, his father promised him he would follow the special rules the judge made. And even though he was a little annoyed at first, he thanked Newton for writing to him and not keeping his feelings and thoughts inside.

♥ The judge told the knight that he must not drink alcohol in front of the children. This was a special rule.

♥ Did the judge make any special rules that your parents are supposed to follow? (Such as, no drinking or using drugs around the children, no spanking, or to stay a certain distance from the other parent's house, or to have someone else with them when they visit you, or to not say bad things about the other parent in front of you? Are there special rules about allowing each parent to have time with you, or about what time each parent is supposed to pick you up and bring you back?)

♥ What would you do if your parents disobeyed the judge's rule?

Newton was glad when his parents told him what was going on. He liked to know ahead of time when he was going to be at each parent's home. He liked to be able to plan ahead and know where and when he was going to be spending holidays.

He liked celebrating each holiday twice, even his birthday! He knew that even though his parents were getting divorced, they still loved him!

♥ Newton liked to be able to look at the calendar and see when he was going to be at each parent's house.

♥ Is there a calendar you can look at to know when you are going to be with each parent?

♥ Where would you like that calendar posted?

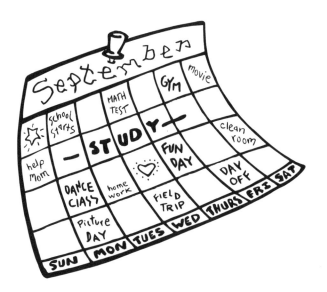

ARLETTA

Arletta was happy to see that her cat had a wonderful warm bed at her father's home. And she was thrilled with her new pet dolphin at her mother's. She wrote stories about adventures she imagined with both of her pets. She put the pictures she drew of her imaginary adventures on her bedroom wall, so she could look at them.

She liked celebrating the underwater holidays of the tides and full moons. She likes celebrating the holidays on the mountain of the seasons and harvests. She especially liked celebrating her birthday at each house.

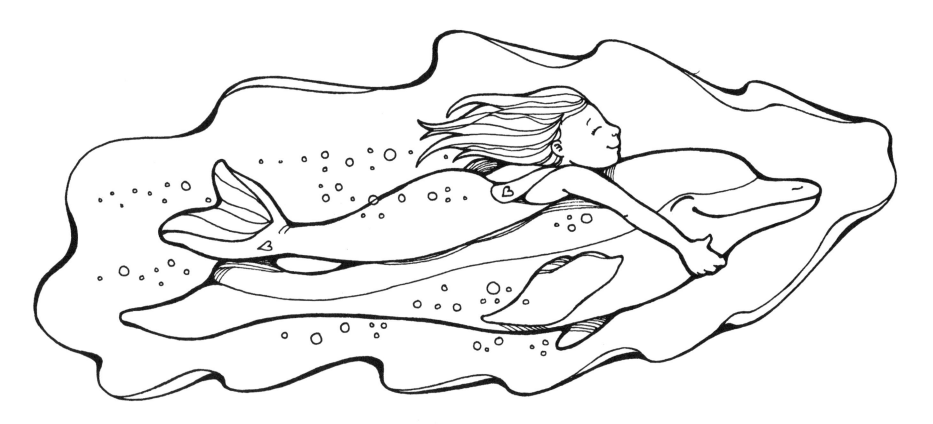

♥ It can be hard to learn to celebrate holidays differently. Arletta found holidays she liked at each of her parent's homes.

♥ How are holidays celebrated differently now that your parents are divorced? (How do you think they may be celebrated differently now?)

♥ How do you celebrate your birthday now? (How would you like to celebrate your birthday after the divorce?)

Arletta still missed the other parent when she was at the other one's home. She wrote letters and made cards for the parent she was missing. She would also always call before she went to bed and say goodnight to the parent she was missing.

Arletta learned that it was O.K. for people to feel sad, even to cry. Sometimes crying can make even grown-ups feel better. And the sad feelings do get better. She began to realize that her parents could decide to live apart, and still always love her. She knew they would always love her no matter what changes happened in life.

Her grandmother also told her, "You are always you no matter what your parents do. And **you** are always lovable."

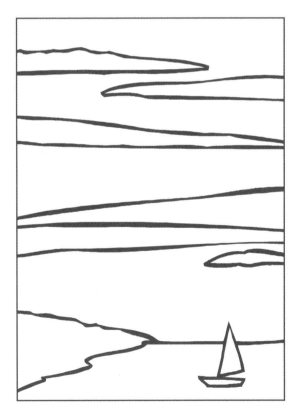

♥ Arletta learned she was always lovable, no matter what.

♥ Draw a picture of you being loved by both parents, even though they are divorced.

Constance, Newton, Arletta and Spartacus each have their own feelings about their parents' divorce. And each child has found different ways to handle his or her feelings. Each one has also found things to like about the new homes. But most importantly, they can all say, "My parents still love me even though they're getting divorced."

Further Reading For Kids:

Dinosaurs Divorce, A Guide For Changing Families, by Laurene Krasny Brown and Marc Brown

How It Feels When Parents Divorce, by Jill Krementz

How To Survive Your Parent's Divorce: Kids' Advice to Kids, by Gayle Kimball

The Boys and Girls Book About Divorce, by Richard A. Gardner, M.D.

The Divorce Workbook, by Sally Blakeslee Ives, Ph.D., David Fassler, M.D., Michele Lash, Med., A.T.R.

When Someone in the Family Drinks Too Much, by Richard Langsen

Why Are We Getting a Divorce? by Peter Mayle

Will Dad Ever Move Back Home? by Paula Z. Hogan, Dora Leder

It's Not Your Fault, KoKo Bear, by Vicki Lansky

I Don't Want to Talk About It, by Jeanie Franz Ransom

Mama and Daddy Bear's Divorce, by Cornelia Spelman

Further Reading For Parents:

Children of Divorce, A Developmental Approach to Residence and Visitation, by Mitchell A. Baris, Ph.D. and Carla B. Garrity, Ph.D

Compassionate Child-Rearing, by Robert W. Firestone, Ph.D.

Custody Chaos, Personal Peace: Sharing Custody with an Ex Who's Driving You Crazy, by Jeffrey Wittmann

Crazy Time: Surviving Divorce, by Abigail Trafford

Creative Divorce, by Mel Kranzler

Divorce Poison: Protecting the Parent-Child Bond from a Vindictive Ex, by Richard Warshak

Fathering, Strengthening Connection With Your Child No Matter Where You Are, by Will Glennon

For The Sake of the Children, How To Share Your Children With Your Ex-spouse In Spite Of Your Anger, by Kris Kline and Stephen Pew, Ph.D.

401 Ways To Get Your Kids To Work At Home, by Bonnie Runyan McCullough and Susan Walker Monson

Healing the Wounds of Divorce, by Barbra Leahy Shelemon

How To Survive The Loss of a Love, by Melba Cosgrove, Peter McWilliams, Harlod H. Bloomfield

How To Talk So Kids Will Listen and Listen So Kids Will Talk, by Adele Faber and Elaine Mazlish

How to Win as a Stepfamily, by Visher and Visher

In Praise Of Single Parents, by Shoshonan Alexander

Joint Custody With a Jerk: Raising a Child With an Uncooperative Ex, A Hands-on Practical Guide, by Ross Corcoran

Keys To Single Parenting, by Carl Pickhardt, Ph.D.

Making It As A Stepparent, by Berman

Mars and Venus Starting Over: A Practical Guide for Finding Love Again After a Painful Breakup, Divorce, or the Loss of a Loved One, by John Gray

Mom's House, Dad's House, by I. Ricci

New Beginnings, Skills For Single Parents and Stepfamily Parents, Parents' Manual, by Don Dinkmeyer, Gary D. Mckay and Joyce L. Mckay

Raising Children In A Socially Toxic Environment, by James Garbarino

Siblings Without Rivalry, How To Help Your Children Live Together So You Can Live Too, by Adele Faber and Elaine Mazlish

Simple Abundance, A Daybook of Comfort and Joy, by Sarah Ban Breathnach

Step by Stepparenting, by James D. Ecker

Stepfamilies, Myths And Realities, by Emily B. Visher, Ph.D. and John S. Visher, M.D.

Successful Single Parenting, by Gary Richmond

Surviving the Breakup: How Children and Parents Cope with Divorce, by J. S. Wallerstein and J. B. Kelly

The Complete Single Mother, by Andrea Engber and Leah Klungness, Ph.D.

The One Minute Father, by Spencer Johnson, M.D.

The Optimistic Child, by Seligman

The Parents Book About Divorce, by R.A. Gardner

The Single Mother's Book, by Joan Anderson

The Single Mother's Companion, Essays And Stories By Women, edited by Marsha R. Leslie

The Single Parent Family, Living Happily in a Changing World, by Marge Kennedy and Janet Spencer King

The Tao of Motherhood, by Vimala McClure

Vicki Lansky's Divorce Book For Parents, by Vicky Lansky

When Anger Hurts Your Kids, a parent's guide, by McKay, Fanning, Paleg and Landis

Where's Daddy? by Claudette Wassil-Grimm, M.Ed.

You're A Stepparent...Now What?, by Joseph Cerquone

Other resources for families going through divorce

Al-anon, Ala-teen, Ala-preteen   888-425-2666
(Support for family members and friends dealing with an alcoholic)

Alcoholics Anonymous (AA)   www.alcoholics-anonymous.org

ACES (Association for Children for Enforcement of Support)   www.childsupport-aces.org

Co-dependents Anonymous (Co-Da)   www.codependents.org
(Support for persons who are painfully invested in the behavior of another person(s)

Child Abuse Hotline   800-422-4453

Crisis Intervention   800-999-9999

Debtors Anonymous   www.debtorsanonymous.org

Local places of worship   Check local Saturday newspaper and phone book

Making Lemonade, the Single Parent Network   www.makinglemonade.com

Marijuana Anonymous   800-766-6779

National Victims Resource Center (Battery/ rape)   800-627-6872 • www.victims-services.org/7resources/national_resources.asp

National Center for Missing and Exploited Children   800-843-5678

Nar-anon   http://nar-anon.org/index.html
(Support for family and friends of addicts)

Narcotics Anonymous   www.na.org

Nicotine Anonymous   800-642-0666 • www.nicotine-anonymous.org

Overeaters Anonymous   www.oa.org

Sex Addicts Anonymous   http://saa-recovery.org

S-Anon   www.sanon.org

Single Rose, Resources for Single Mothers   www.singlerose.com

About the author

Lois V. Nightingale, Ph. D. is a licensed Clinical Psychologist, and licensed Marriage, Child and Family Therapist in California. She has been helping individuals and families for over twenty-five years. She is also the director of the Nightingale Center in Yorba Linda, California.

She is a nationally recognized speaker and an award-winning writer. She has made many professional appearances on local, national and international television helping to educate parents and teach better ways of communicating among family members. She is widely sought as a speaker for conferences, workshops, retreats, churches and temples.

As a divorced single mother of two children, she realized the importance of a story that children could relate to, but one that also was instructional, a story that would teach coping skills and better ways to handle the confusion of divorce and give children an opportunity to express their feelings.

It is her goal to help families find resources to assist them through changes. She believes that if children receive support, encouragement, and a safe place to express their feelings during times of difficult change and loss, many of the negative long-term effects of these childhood disruptions can be avoided. Children can learn they are lovable and strong. And she feels that parents have a responsibility to model for their children (even in the face of adversity and change) there is always an opportunity to become more caring, compassionate and self-assured individuals.

Dr. Nightingale lives in Yorba Linda, California with her two children.

A page so kids can write to the author.

What would you want other kids to know who are just now starting to go through a divorce?

In what ways was your parents' divorce different from that of one of your friends?

What are you most proud of, in yourself, as you went through your parents' divorce?

Children may send responses to: Lois V. Nightingale, Ph.D., 16960 E. Bastanchury Rd Suite. J, Yorba Linda, Ca. 92886

To order more copies of this book for a friend, or other children in your family:

Please include for each copy of *My Parents Still Love Me Even Though They're Getting Divorced* (order #B100):
per copy $14.95 (US) number of copies _____   total   _____
Within Calif. please include 7.75% tax ($1.16 per book)   total tax   _____
Shipping and handling: $3.00 first book ($1.75 each additional book) total   _____
($6.00 if outside the USA)
Total amount of check or money order enclosed: _____

If paying by Master Card or Visa:
 • Call toll free: 800-898-8426
 • Or send fax to: 714-993-3467
 • Or include card number, expiration date, signature and send to:

Nightingale Rose Publications
16960 E. Bastanchury Rd. Suite J
Yorba Linda, Ca. 92886